W9-BZD-408

Tom Sawyer lives with his Aunt Polly in the sleepy village of St Petersburg on the banks of the Mississippi. Tom and his friend, Huckleberry Finn, have many adventures together but their lives are changed one night when they visit the graveyard and see something strange happening there.

Mark Twain's original Adventures of Tom Sawyer was written over one hundred years ago. In this version the story is faithfully retold and beautifully illustrated for young readers.

British Library Cataloguing in Publication Data
Sibley, Raymond
   Tom Sawyer.—(Ladybird children's classics; 39)
   I. Title   II. Twain, Mark. Adventures of Tom Sawyer
   III. Gabbey, Terry
   823'.914[J]   PZ7
   ISBN 0-7214-0977-6

First edition

Published by Ladybird Books Ltd Loughborough Leicestershire UK
Ladybird Books Inc Lewiston Maine 04240 USA

© LADYBIRD BOOKS LTD MCMLXXXVI
All rights reserved. No part of this publication may be reproduced, stored in a retrieval system, or transmitted in any form or by any means, electronic, mechanical, photo-copying, recording or otherwise, without the prior consent of the copyright owner.

Printed in England

TOM
SAWYER

by Mark Twain

retold by Raymond Sibley
illustrated by Terry Gabbey

Ladybird Books

It was mid-afternoon in the deep south of America and the village of St Petersburg, near the Mississippi, was baking in the sun.

Aunt Polly was sitting by an open window, knitting. Soon the balmy summer air, the stillness, the scent of flowers and the murmuring of the bees made her nod off to sleep.

Outside the house Tom was looking at a board-fence thirty yards long and nine feet high. He had with him a bucket of whitewash and a long-handled brush. Aunt Polly had given him the job as an afternoon's punishment for fighting. The piece he had done already looked very small indeed compared with what was left. His spirits were very low. It would take hours to finish, maybe until dark.

Just then Ben Rogers came into sight. As he reached Tom, he slowed down. Tom pretended not to notice him.

'Hello, you got to work?' asked Ben.

'Work, Ben! What do you call work?' said Tom.

'Why, ain't *that* work?' replied Ben.

Tom carried on whitewashing. 'Maybe it is, but it suits me, Ben.'

'Come on, you don't mean you *like* it, Tom?'

'Like it? Why not? A boy doesn't get a chance to whitewash a fence every day.' Ben watched every move as Tom swept the brush daintily back and forth, stopping every now and then to add a touch here and a touch there.

Ben got more and more interested. 'Say, Tom. Let me do a little.'

'No I can't, Ben,' said Tom. 'You see, Aunt Polly is very particular about this fence and it's right on the street.' Ben frowned.

'If it was at the back she wouldn't mind, and I wouldn't mind either,' said Tom. 'You see, I'm the only boy who can do it properly.'

'Oh, shucks. I'll be real careful, Tom,' said Ben. 'She won't be able to tell, honest.' So Tom gave Ben the brush and sat himself down to watch, eating the apple Ben had given him.

Soon other boys came along and when Ben became tired, Billy Fisher gave Tom a kite so that *he* could be allowed to take over. When Billy Fisher began to weaken, Johnny Miller gave Tom some blue bottle-glass so he could carry on next.

By this time boys were standing in line waiting their turns and Tom had collected from them marbles, keys, a Jew's harp, chalk, glass-stoppers, tadpoles, toy soldiers, a brass door-knob, a knife and many other things.

When the fence was finished they started again and went on until the whitewash had all been used up. Then Tom went back into the house. 'May I go to play now, Aunt?' he asked.

'Have you finished the fence?' she replied.

'Yes. It's all done.'

She didn't believe him and went outside to look for herself. 'Well, I never! You *can* work Tom, when you have a mind to, but that's not often. Go along and play but don't be late back.'

Tom walked around the block
and through a muddy alley by the back of his
aunt's cow stable and on towards the village.
As he passed by the house where the Thatchers
lived he saw a girl in the garden. He had never
seen her before. She was a lovely blue-eyed
creature with plaited hair, and she was dressed
in a white summer frock. He fell in love with her
immediately and forgot about every other girl at
the same moment.

The girl turned and looked towards him so he
pretended not to notice but did some gymnastic
stunts to impress her. As he glanced at her
again he saw that she was walking back to the
house. He leaned on the fence. She halted on
the steps to the house and then, as her foot
touched the threshold, she tossed a flower over
the fence and went in.

Tom ran to the spot, made sure no one in the
street was watching, put his bare foot over the
flower and picked it up between his toes. Then
he hopped around the corner before putting the
flower next to his heart, or where he thought his
heart was. He hung about the fence until it got
dark but the girl did not come out again, so he
returned home.

The next day was Sunday. After breakfast Aunt Polly held family worship with prayers, followed by a grim sermon. Then Tom had to wash and dress for Sunday school. He put on his Sunday best clothes but lost his temper when his cousin Mary made him wear shoes, for he liked to go barefoot.

Sunday school hours were from nine o'clock to half past ten, followed by a church service.

The whole class performed badly at their lessons and had to be corrected. When Mr Walters, the Superintendent, stood in front of the pulpit to speak to them, the children quarrelled, fidgeted, whispered and played games.

The whispering had started when Lawyer Thatcher had come in with visitors, including a lady who was leading a child. It was the pretty girl Tom had seen the previous evening.

Mr Walters introduced one of the men as Judge Thatcher, the brother of their own Lawyer Thatcher. There was a long silence. Mr Walters dearly wanted to present a Bible prize but he thought that no pupils had enough merit-tickets to qualify. These were tickets awarded to pupils who did very good work.

Now Tom had for some time traded other things for merit-tickets and had enough to qualify for a Bible. The Superintendent was astonished as Tom presented a full range of yellow, red and blue tickets. Never in ten years could Tom Sawyer have earned them himself. But there was nothing Mr Walters could do about it.

Tom was called up to sit near the Judge. All those children who had given or traded their tickets to Tom watched in stunned amazement. Mr Walters presented the prize but said very little in praise, for he knew that somehow the boy had obtained his merit-tickets dishonestly. Even Tom quaked when he was introduced to the Judge, mainly because he had heard that he was the father of the little girl that Tom loved.

'You are a fine boy,' said the Judge. 'A fine manly little fellow. You must have worked very hard at your lessons to have earned this Bible. Tell us the names of the first two disciples of Jesus.'

Tom looked alarmed and remained silent.

'Now,' repeated the Judge, 'tell me. The names of the first two disciples were—'

'David and Goliath,' muttered Tom.
Mr Walters' heart sank within him.

At half past ten the church bell began to ring and the children joined their parents to be under supervision for the morning service. Tom sat with Aunt Polly, his half-brother, Sid and Cousin Mary. He was ill at ease and his mind wandered as the minister droned on monotonously.

After some time Tom remembered that he had a large black beetle in the small box in his pocket. Slowly he reached for the box and opened it. The beetle fell into the aisle.

Presently a stray dog came in and sat down near it. The dog began to nod off to sleep and gradually his chin dropped until it touched the beetle. There was a sharp yelp of pain from the dog as the beetle bit into his chin. The dog jumped at it and then grew tired, forgetting about the beetle entirely. He yawned, sighed and sat down on it, by mistake!

There was a wild yelp of agony and the dog ran up the aisle with the beetle attached behind, biting him at every step. He raced over the altar, flew down another aisle still yelping, jumped up at the doors and finally escaped through a window.

By this time the whole congregation was red-faced and suffocating with suppressed laughter. The sermon continued but it was a failure as choked laughter could be heard every few seconds.

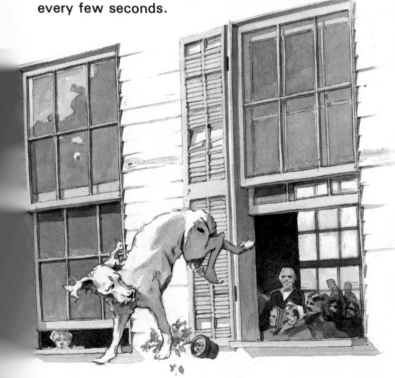

Tom went home in a cheerful mood thinking that divine service was much better when there was a bit of variety in it.

Monday morning found Tom Sawyer miserable, because it began another week's slow suffering in school. As he made his way wearily along the lane he met Huckleberry Finn, son of the town drunkard. All the mothers of the town dreaded and hated Huckleberry because he was lazy, vulgar and lawless.

The boys envied him but were under strict orders neither to mix with him nor to copy his behaviour.

Huckleberry was always dressed in the cast-off clothes of full-grown men. He slept on doorsteps in fine weather and in empty barrels when it was wet. He did not have to go to school or church, call anybody master or obey anyone.

He could fish or swim when he liked, for as long as he liked. Nobody stopped him fighting and he could stay up as late as he pleased. He never had to wash or put on clean clothes and he could swear whenever he chose.

Tom liked Huck and talked to him for some time and this made him late for school. However he strode briskly into the schoolroom, put his hat on a peg and sat down.

The teacher watched him from his high chair. 'Thomas Sawyer!' he bellowed. 'Come here and explain why you are late.'

Tom was about to tell a lie when he saw the new girl he loved, and beside her was the only empty place on the girls' side of the schoolroom, so he said, 'I stopped to talk with Huckleberry Finn!'

The noise of study ceased and the master stared at him. 'You—you did what?' he said.

'Stopped to talk with Huckleberry Finn.'

'Come here, Thomas Sawyer,' said the master, sternly. 'Take off your jacket and hand me that switch.'

After Tom had received a severe beating the master said, 'Now, sir, go and sit with the *girls*!'

Tom sat down on the end of the pine bench near the girl whom he had worshipped from afar. She moved herself away from him with a toss of her head. Tom sat still.

'My name's Tom Sawyer. What's yours?' he whispered.

'Becky Thatcher,' she replied.

Tom began to write on his slate, hiding the words from the girl. But she begged to see.

'Oh, it ain't anything,' he said.

'Yes it is.'

'You don't want to see it.'

'Please, Tom, let me.'

'You'll tell!'

'No, I won't, Tom.' And she put her small hand on his hand. He pretended to resist but gradually let his hand slip until she could read the words: *I love you.*

'Oh, you bad thing!' she said, and smacked his hand, but she blushed and looked very pleased.

At that moment Tom felt a hard grip on his
ear and a lifting sensation. In that vice-like grip
the master led him back to his own place.
Tom's ear tingled but his heart was light. When
school broke up at noon, Tom ran to Becky
Thatcher. 'Put on your bonnet,' he whispered,
'and let on you're going home, then turn down
through the lane and come back.'

By the time they reached the school they had
it all to themselves. Tom was full of happiness
as they sat down to talk.

'Becky, was you ever engaged?'

'No. What is it like?'

'Why it ain't like anything. You just tell a boy
you won't ever have anybody but him. Then you
kiss.'

'Kiss?' said Becky. 'What do you kiss for?'

'Well, they always do that,' replied Tom.

'Everybody?'

'Yes. Everybody that's in love with each other.'

Tom passed his arm around her waist and whispered in her ear, 'I love you. Now you whisper it to me.'

After a few seconds she bent timidly over Tom until her breath stirred his curls and whispered, 'I—love—you!'

Then she sprang away and ran around the desks with Tom after her until he trapped her in a corner. 'Now Becky, it's all over but the kiss. Please Becky.'

By and by she gave in and Tom kissed her. 'Now Becky,' he said. 'You ain't ever to love anybody but me and you ain't ever to marry anybody but me, *never*.'

'I'll never love anybody but you, Tom and I'll never marry anybody but you, and you ain't ever to marry anybody but me, either.'

'Of course, Becky,' promised Tom. 'It means as we always walk together, when there ain't anybody looking, and I choose you at parties and you choose me, because we're engaged.'

'It sounds ever so nice.'

'It is,' replied Tom. 'Why, me and Amy Lawrence—'

The big eyes looked at him. 'Oh, Tom. Then I ain't the first you been engaged to?'

'Don't cry, Becky, I don't like her any more.' He tried to put his arm round her but she pushed him away, every time. She continued sobbing and when he offered her a marble she knocked it to the floor.

Tom marched out of the schoolhouse, towards the hills and decided not to return for afternoon school. After some minutes Becky went to the door and called his name but he was not in sight.

After wandering the countryside until it was almost dark, Tom returned home. At half past nine he and Sid were sent to bed as usual. Sid was soon asleep but Tom lay awake, for that morning he had arranged with Huckleberry Finn to go to the churchyard at midnight.

At about half past eleven Tom got dressed and crept outside to meet Huck by the woodshed. The two boys reached the tall grass of the graveyard shortly before midnight. The wind moaned through the trees and Tom felt uneasy. Their talk went in stops and starts. Presently Tom seized his companion's arm and said, 'Listen! Can you hear anything? There, again!'

'Lord, Tom, they're coming!' whispered Huck. 'What shall we do?'

'Think they'll see us, Huck?'

'Yes. All devils can see in the dark. I'm all of a shiver. I wish I hadn't come.'

Three vague figures approached through the gloom, one holding a lighted lantern.

'Why, that's Muff Potter's voice,' said Huck. 'I bet he's drunk again, as usual, the old rip! Who are the other two?'

'One's the half-breed, Injun Joe,' replied Tom, 'and the other is young Dr Robinson.'

The men had a handbarrow and two spades with them and after Dr Robinson had put the lantern at the head of Hoss Williams' grave, Potter and Injun Joe took up the spades and began to dig up the coffin. Tom and Huckleberry were so close that they could have touched the doctor as he stood watching the men dig.

When the men reached the coffin, they prised the lid off, put the body on the barrow, covered it with a blanket and secured it with a rope. Potter cut off the end bits of the rope with his spring-knife.

'There,' he said. 'Now just pay us another five each, Doctor, or we don't move the body any further.'

'What do you mean?' exclaimed Dr Robinson. 'You asked for your money in advance and I have paid you.'

'Yes,' snarled Injun Joe, 'and five years ago when I came to your house for food, you said that I was no good and your father had me jailed for begging. I swore I'd get even, so pay up!'

   The doctor struck out suddenly, knocking
Injun Joe to the ground and Potter dropped his
knife to grapple with him. The doctor felled
Potter with a heavy piece of wood.

   Injun Joe picked up the knife and ran
forward, pushing it deep into the doctor's chest.
Dr Robinson slumped across Potter, covering
him with blood.

'*Now* we are even,' Injun Joe muttered. Then he went through the doctor's pockets and put the bloody knife into Potter's hand. After a few minutes Potter moaned and sat up, pushing the body from him and at the same time dropping the knife with a shudder.

'Why did you stab him?' asked Injun Joe, without moving.

'I never,' said Potter, trembling. 'I know I was drunk and my head's in a muddle, but I didn't, did I, Joe?'

'Well, he hit you with the wood, then you got up and knifed him just as he knocked you down again.'

'I didn't know what I was doing,' cried Potter. 'Joe, don't tell on me, I always liked you and stood up for you.'

'Don't worry, Muff Potter. You were always square with me. I won't go back on you.'

They departed together leaving the murdered doctor, the blanketed corpse, the lidless coffin and the open grave.

Tom and Huck also departed, running at full speed to the village, speechless with horror at what they had seen. At last they stopped for breath, at some old ruined buildings. 'Tom, we *got* to keep mum,' whispered Huck. 'If Injun Joe finds out we saw, he'll kill us both.'

When Tom crept back into his own bed it was nearly dawn.

By midday the whole village was talking about the murder and Muff Potter's knife being found near the body. Then things happened at breathtaking speed. Potter was arrested and put into a shed that served as a jail. It was unguarded, had a grated window and stood near the marsh at the edge of the village. Injun Joe was questioned and he made a statement but said nothing about the grave robbery before the fight.

Becky Thatcher was away from school in the afternoon and Tom lost interest in everything. Next morning she returned and he began pushing the other boys, throwing caps and generally jumping about to attract her attention, but all she said was, 'Some people think they're mighty smart—always showing off.'

When the bell rang to go into school, Tom turned and walked in the opposite direction. He was gloomy and forsaken.

He met Joe Harper who was also feeling low,
for his mother had whipped him for something
he hadn't done. They walked along together
sorrowfully. After listening to one another they
decided to run away. But first they hunted out
Huckleberry Finn, who seemed keen to go with
them and so the three planned to meet at
midnight, with food, fishing tackle and anything
else they could carry that might come in useful.

Time passed slowly for the rest of the day but
at last midnight came. The three met silently in
the darkness of the village and then they made
for a section of the Mississippi where the river
was very wide. Here they found a raft on which
they put their food and fishing tackle and soon
they were in the middle of the river.

About two hours later the raft ran aground on a small island, so they unloaded, lit a fire, fried some bacon and finally went to sleep in the long grass, but not before their consciences told them that they had been wrong to run away.

The three boys spent the next day exploring the island, swimming, playing games and cooking the fish that they caught from the river. Towards evening they saw a ferry-boat chugging in the distance about a mile from the village. At intervals a cannon was fired from across the water, making a rumble like thunder.

'They do that when somebody's drowned,' said Tom. 'It makes the body come to the top.'

'I wonder who it is?' exclaimed Joe.

They watched in silence until Tom said suddenly, 'It's us! It's us they're looking for.'

They felt like heroes. They were missed. Hearts were breaking on their account. Tears were being shed. They were the talk of the village.

As twilight drew on, the ferry-boat disappeared. The boys were full of vanity over the trouble they were causing. After a fish supper they prepared for a second night outdoors, but Tom and Joe began to worry about the people at home who were suffering.

The following day was much the same; they played, swam and ate. They found turtle eggs and had a fried egg feast that night. But by afternoon the next day Joe Harper was feeling homesick and tearful. Tom felt downcast too but tried hard not to show it. Even Huckleberry looked miserable and that evening they went to sleep in sadness.

Meanwhile back in the village the Harper family and Aunt Polly's family were mourning the death of the boys. When Sunday came the church was full. As the service went on many people sobbed loudly. Nobody noticed when the church door creaked open but the minister raised his streaming eyes from his handkerchief and ceased his pathetic story.

One by one the congregation followed his gaze and then they all rose and stared hard as Tom, Joe and Huck sneaked in from where they had been hiding, listening to their own funeral sermon. Everyone was so pleased to see them alive that the boys' escapade was forgiven but not forgotten.

Not long afterwards Becky and Tom became friends again after a very unusual incident.

Now Mr Dobbins, the schoolmaster, had always wanted to be a doctor but could not afford the training. He had never lost his interest in medicine so when his pupils were hard at work he would take a book on the subject and read it eagerly. He kept it locked in his desk. Every day his pupils had different ideas on what the book was about.

One day when Becky was passing the desk she saw the key in the lock. Nobody was about

so she opened the desk and took out the book.
At that moment Tom came in. She was so
startled that she jumped and tore the page she
was holding.

'Now look what you made me do,' she said
bursting into tears. 'I'll be whipped and I've
never been whipped before.' She ran out, still
crying bitterly.

Afternoon school had been going for an hour
or more before Mr Dobbins unlocked his desk.
'Who tore this book?' he asked.

There was not a sound. The silence seemed to go on forever. The master searched face after face and then began to ask each child in turn. When he reached Becky Thatcher her face had turned white with terror and her hands twitched nervously. 'Rebecca Thatcher, did you tear this book?' asked the master.

Tom sprang to his feet and shouted, 'I done it!'

Tom then received a severe flogging and was commanded to remain at school for two hours after the others had been dismissed. But it was worth it. When finally he left the schoolroom Becky said, 'Tom, how could you be so noble!'

When the school holidays began and Becky Thatcher went away to stay with her parents, it was like a light going out of Tom's life. To make matters worse he had measles for two weeks, during which he felt extra miserable because Muff Potter's trial was getting near. Tom and Huck knew that Muff Potter had often got drunk but he had been generous with the little he had and was always kind and helpful to them.

As there were no guards watching Potter in his prison shed the boys took tobacco and matches and put them through the cell grating. Muff was very grateful. 'You two boys have been mighty good to me,' he said. 'I don't forget, Tom and Huck. Well boys, I done that dreadful thing when I was crazy drunk, and now

I got to hang for it. Lift one another up and let me shake hands with you through the bars. Goodbye.'

Tom went home miserable. Huck felt bad too.

At the end of the second day of the trial it looked bad for Muff Potter as Injun Joe's evidence stood firm and unshaken. There was no doubt what the verdict of the jury would be. Tom knew that there was only one thing to be done. That night he went to the lawyer who was defending Muff Potter and told him everything.

On the third day, evidence piled up against Muff but for some strange reason, unknown to the people in court, his Counsel did not cross-examine any witnesses. At the close of the evidence the Counsel for Potter stood up and said that his client was changing his plea from one of having committed the murder while drunk, to a new one of 'not guilty'. He then called Tom to the witness box and the oath was given. Tom was scared and all the people in the courtroom looked very puzzled.

'Thomas Sawyer,' he said. 'Where were you on the seventeenth of June, about the hour of midnight?'

At first the words would not come; then Tom whispered, 'In the graveyard.'

'Tell the court exactly what you saw, that night.'

Tom began his story with every eye in the room fixed upon him.

When he reached the point where the doctor was stabbed, Injun Joe jumped to his feet, ran across the court, leapt through an open window and soon disappeared from sight.

Tom became the pet of the old and the envy of the young in the village afterwards. His days were good but his nights were full of horror. Injun Joe filled all his dreams. Both Tom and Huck were in the same state of wretchedness and terror. They both felt that they never could draw a safe breath again until Injun Joe was captured. But the slow days drifted on and, as they passed, the boys' fears got lighter and lighter.

Then one Saturday they walked out of the village until they reached an old ruin that was known as 'the haunted house'. It was a weird and grisly place. They crept into an unplastered room, with a broken floor that had weeds growing through it, broken windows and a smashed fireplace. Cobwebs hung down everywhere.

After exploring all the rooms they climbed up the decayed staircase. While they were upstairs they heard someone enter the house. In fright they lay down and looked through the holes in the wooden floor. They were terrified when they saw Injun Joe and another man.

For what seemed like hours the boys lay still. Injun Joe and his partner smashed the planking of the downstairs floor and pulled out a small treasure chest, rusty with age. 'There's thousands of dollars in here,' said Injun Joe.

The two men carried the box towards the river and Tom and Huck, still trembling, went back to the village, wondering how they could get the treasure for themselves.

A few days later Tom heard that Becky Thatcher had come back from staying with her parents. The treasure was put right out of his mind, especially as Becky's mother had arranged a picnic for the following day, which was a Saturday.

At ten o'clock in the morning all the children met outside Lawyer Thatcher's. A few young ladies of eighteen and some young men of twenty or so took charge. Off they went in a steam ferry-boat that had been hired for the occasion.

Sid was sick and Mary had to stay at home to look after him, so Tom was free to spend all his time with Becky as Huck did not go either. The last thing Becky's mother said was, 'You'll be late back, Becky, so perhaps you'd better stay the night with some of the girls that live near the ferry.'

'I'll stay with Susie Harper, Mamma.'

'Very well, Becky, that's fine.'

Three miles below the village the ferry-boat stopped at the mouth of a woody hollow. All the children swarmed ashore. Soon the air was full of shouting and laughter. Next came the picnic feast and after that somebody shouted, 'Who's ready for McDougal's cave?'

Everybody was. Bundles of candles were given out and soon they were exploring the cave. It was romantic and mysterious. Gradually

the children split into smaller groups advancing
about a mile into the cave, blowing out one
another's candles, hiding away and leaping out
until even they became tired and returned to the
ferry-boat. But not Becky and Tom.

When the
two had first
separated from the
other children they had
found themselves in a
beautiful high cavern, the top of which was
covered with bats. The lights disturbed the
creatures and they flew about, one knocking the
candle from Becky's grasp. As the bats
swooped on them the children ran hand-in-hand,
first into one passage and then another. Finally
they sat down beside an underground lake.

The place was silent.

'Tom, I can't hear the others,' said Becky. 'We had better go back.'

'Right, but we'd better try to keep away from the bats.' They walked for a very long time, then Tom said, 'I'm sorry, Becky. I can't find the way.'

Becky began to cry when she realised that they were lost. Tom sat beside her and put his arms round her. In his pocket he had just four pieces of candle left. They talked and walked and rested. After some hours, tired out, Becky slept. When she awoke they ate pieces of picnic cake that they had put into their pockets.

'Becky, can you bear it if I tell you something?' asked Tom. She nodded. 'We'll have to stay put near this spring of drinking water as this is our last piece of candle. Soon they will miss us and come to look for us.'

'But, Tom, it will be Sunday morning before Mother finds out that I was not at Mrs Harper's,' whispered Becky. Their last bit of candle melted away and they were in total darkness.

When Tom awoke he had no idea whether it was night or day. Becky still slept. Tom thought he heard a sound, but he was not sure. There it was again! He took his kite-line from his pocket and tied one end to a rock and moved slowly along a passage, unwinding the line as he groped along. He got down on his knees and felt every inch of the way.

As he turned a corner he saw, about twenty yards away, the figure of a man holding a candle. He was scratching a mark on the cave wall as if to show where he had hidden something. Tom stood up. The man turned. It was Injun Joe. Tom was scared, but Injun Joe seemed just as shocked for in an instant he moved out of sight, leaving Tom in darkness.

As Tom stood there, shaking, he heard Becky call out so he went back to her. He did not mention Injun Joe as he didn't want to frighten her.

After church on the morning following the picnic, Becky's mother asked Mrs Harper, 'Is Becky still sleeping? I expect she is tired after the caves.'

'Becky?' said Mrs Harper, puzzled.

'Didn't she stay with you last night?'

'Why, no.'

Becky's mother turned pale. Just then Aunt Polly passed by and enquired where Tom had stayed as he hadn't been home. Children were questioned. Nobody had noticed them on the ferry-boat on the homeward trip. Slowly it dawned on everyone that they must have got lost in the cave.

Soon two hundred men were making for the spot by road and river, but after three dreadful days and nights there was no news of Becky and Tom.

By Tuesday afternoon the village of St Petersburg was in mourning. The lost children had not been found. Prayers had been said for them and searchers had given up all hope of finding them.

In the middle of the night there was shouting in the streets, 'Turn out! Turn out! They are found.' Lights went up everywhere and nobody went back to bed.

It seemed that as Tom had prowled around with his kite-line he had seen a speck of light. After much scrambling and falling over rocks the two had squeezed out through a small hole, right next to the river. Some men saw them and couldn't believe that the children had wandered five miles down river from the main entrance.

Becky and Tom were put to bed to recover from their ordeal and they stayed there for a week. Huck was also sick at the time and being looked after by Widow Douglas, a kind and good-natured person who lived in the village.

About a fortnight after the rescue Tom heard that Judge Thatcher had sealed the cave entrance with an iron door and double lock. He had done this the day after Becky and Tom had returned, so no other children would ever get lost. Tom immediately ran to see Judge Thatcher. 'Oh, Judge, Injun Joe's in the cave!' he told him.

But when the men reached McDougal's cave and unlocked the door, Injun Joe was dead. They buried him near the mouth of the cave.

The morning after the funeral, Huck spoke to Tom about the treasure. 'I always knew we'd never find it,' he said.

'But Huck, it's in the cave! I can show you. It's near the spring where I saw Injun Joe.'

'We could float a skiff down to there, Tom!'

'Yes, but we'll need some food, two or three small bags, three or four kite-strings, candles and some of those big lucifer-matches.'

Just after noon they set off in a borrowed skiff. Sure enough, Tom took Huck straight to the small opening. They fixed the first of the kite-lines and armed with lighted candles moved slowly to the spring where Becky and Tom had rested. Nearby, they found Injun Joe's mark on the cave wall and beneath it a rock covered with candle grease.

Under the rock was some rubble and beneath the rubble the treasure-box. It was heavy. Tom could just lift it with difficulty. So they emptied the box and put the coins in the bags they had with them. The rest was easy. They returned by skiff to the village.

After they had broken the news to Aunt Polly, Widow Douglas and Judge Thatcher, the money was counted. It amounted to twelve thousand dollars.

'Huck and I are sharing half each,' said Tom. Widow Douglas invested Huck's money and Judge Thatcher invested Tom's at Aunt Polly's request.

Widow Douglas looked after Huck but he was not sure he liked to be clean. But Tom and Huck took comfort in the thought that when they were men, they could become famous as robbers or pirates; then Aunt Polly and Widow Douglas would be proud of them.